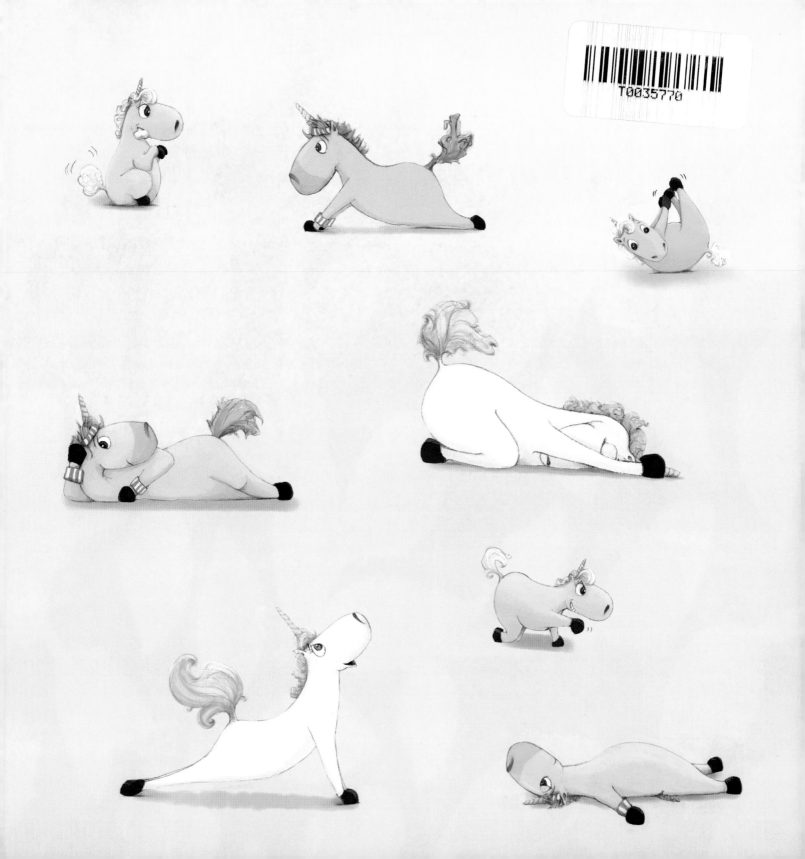

For Julia Ruocco Vitella, a guiding light
on the path that is yoga
—Gina and Bree

☆

For Mimi
—Jen

Text Copyright © 2020 Gina Cascone and Bryony Williams Sheppard
Illustration Copyright © 2020 Jennifer Sattler

SLEEPING BEAR PRESS™
2395 South Huron Parkway, Suite 200
Ann Arbor, MI 48104
www.sleepingbearpress.com

Printed and bound in the United States.

10 9 8 7 6 5 4 3 2

Library of Congress Cataloging-in-Publication Data

Names: Cascone, Gina, author. | Williams Sheppard, Bryony, author. |
Sattler, Jennifer Gordon, illustrator.
Title: Unicorn yoga / written by Gina Cascone and Bryony
Williams Sheppard ; illustrated by Jennifer Sattler.
Description: Ann Arbor, Michigan : Sleeping Bear Press, [2020] | Audience:
Ages 4-8 | Summary: "Through easy-to-follow instructions, a unicorn yogi leads
readers through a ten-pose class. Back matter provides additional information
on yoga, as well as tips on mindfulness"— Provided by publisher.
Identifiers: LCCN 2020006359 | ISBN 9781534111066 (hardcover)
Subjects: LCSH: Hatha yoga—Juvenile literature.
Classification: LCC RA781.7 C389 2020 | DDC 613.7/046—dc23
LC record available at https://lccn.loc.gov/2020006359

UNICORN Yoga

Gina Cascone & Bryony Williams Sheppard ✰ Illustrated by Jennifer Sattler

PUBLISHED BY SLEEPING BEAR PRESS

EASY POSE

Welcome to Unicorn Yoga.

Yoga is for everybody . . . and for *every* body. Big, small, young, old. The practice makes us strong and graceful.

We begin by sitting on our mats, crisscross applesauce. In Easy Pose, we are mindful and centered. *Om.*

COW POSE

☆ Roll up onto your hands and knees and take a deep breath in through your nose.

☆ Drop your belly, lift your tail, and look up.

This is the *moo*velous Cow Pose.

CAT POSE

☆ Breathe out.

☆ Now push the ground away and arch your back.

You are—*meow*—in Cat Pose. Cat-Cow will help us move with our breath as we continue our practice.

Breathe in. Breathe out.

TIGER POSE

Your cat becomes a Tiger Pose. No, it's not time to roar, but it is time to build balance and flexibility.

☆ Extend one arm out as far as it can go and kick your opposite leg back.

☆ Then touch your knee and elbow together under your tummy.

☆ Now the other side.

Breathe in. Breathe out.

CHILD'S POSE

- ☆ Sit back on your feet.

- ☆ Slowly bend forward, touching your forehead to your mat.

- ☆ Stretch your arms and fingertips out, keeping your palms on the ground.

Child's Pose will help you concentrate.
It always works for me!

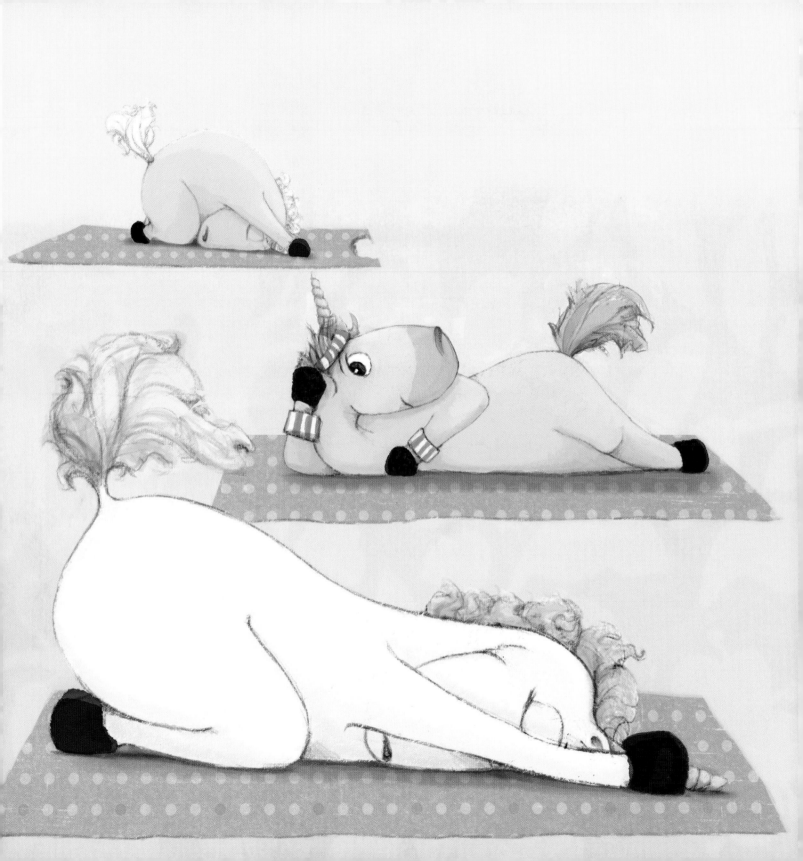

DOWNWARD-FACING DOG POSE

☆ Tuck your toes down and press hard into your fingers.

☆ Lift your tail high into the air and straighten your legs.

You are an upside-down V, or in Downward-Facing Dog Pose. *Woof!* Do you feel the energy rushing through your body?

FORWARD-FOLD POSE

☆ Tiptoe forward until your feet are between your hands.

☆ Hang freely and make this pose your own.

☆ Touch the ground.

☆ Put your nose to your knees.

☆ Wrap your arms around your legs.

Any way you do it, you are strengthening your legs in a Forward-Fold Pose.

Breathe in. Breathe out.

PLANK POSE

☆ Plant your hands on your mat and hop or step back as far as you can with both feet.

☆ Make a straight line from your ankles to the tip of your head.

You are in Plank Pose. You might feel as if your arms and legs are doing all the work, but focus on your core (abdominal region) and spine as they get nice and strong. Gosh, I could stay this way all day!

Breathe in. Breathe out.

COBRA
POSE

☆ Lower your belly to your mat and point your toes behind you.

It's time to *sssslither* into Cobra Pose.

☆ Keep your hands under your shoulders and your arms bent, slowly lifting your head and chest.

Breathe in. Breathe out.

UPWARD-FACING DOG POSE

☆ Straighten your arms and legs.

☆ Hold your body up with your hands and the tops of your feet.

Throw your head back and howl at the moon in Upward-Facing Dog Pose.

RELAXATION POSE

Finally, it's time to take our rest.

☆ Lying on our backs without moving a muscle in Relaxation Pose, we find stillness and peace.

☆ Quiet body. Quiet mind. We reflect on our practice and gather the energy to move through our day.

Namaste.

Let's do this again tomorrow!

Breathe in. Breathe out.

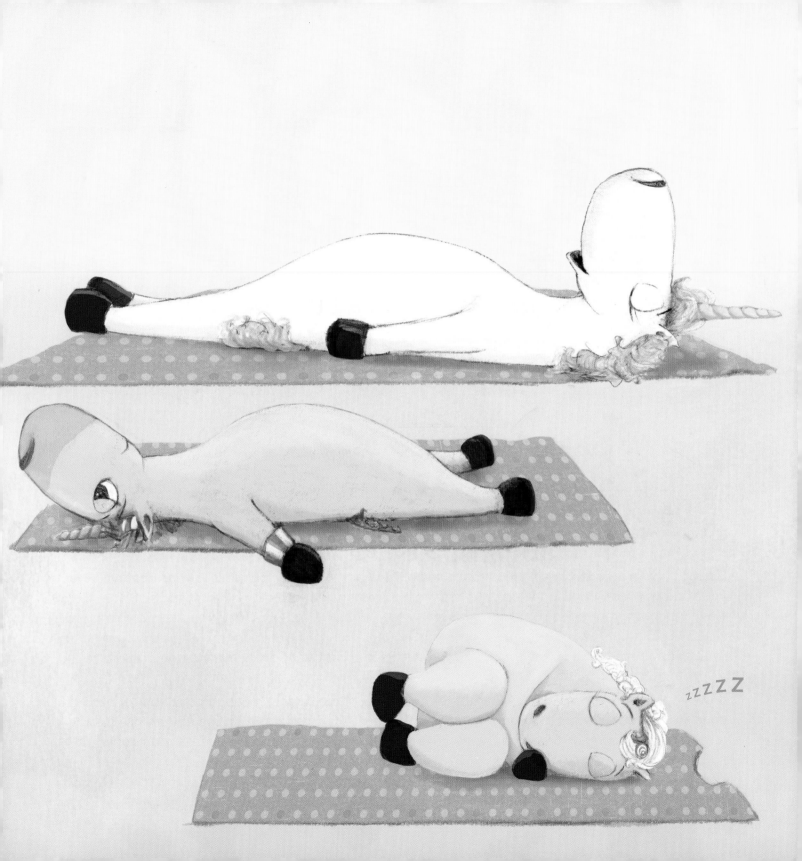

zzZZZ

Yoga is good for everybody and *every body*—even unicorns!

The word *yoga* means "to unite," or to be connected to all things in the universe. This is why so many of the postures imitate nature and animals. We look to the flexibility of the cat and the playfulness of the dog. As we move from position to position, our focus remains on steady and purposeful breathing to keep mind and body working in harmony.

Yoga's ultimate goal is to create a sense of peace, self-awareness, compassion, and community. Balance, strength, flexibility, and good posture are also developed while practicing. Yoga increases blood flow and brings more oxygen through the body, energizing it—strong body, strong mind.

Yoga is also the perfect brain break! Studies show that brain breaks help us focus and retain information. Taking time to energize and refresh creates greater opportunities for learning.

Off the mat and into the world!

The most important skill that yoga gives us is mindful breathing. By learning to control our breath, we also learn to control our emotions. If we practice these calming exercises for just a few minutes every day, we will be able to use them successfully when we need them the most.

Count on your breath: Sit in a comfortable position or lie on your back. Rest your arms alongside your body or rest your hands on your stomach to feel the breath as it goes in and out. Breathe in slowly through your nose as you count silently to yourself. *One. Two. Three. Four.* Hold your breath. *One. Two.* Exhale slowly. *One. Two. Three. Four.* Pause. *One. Two.* Begin again by inhaling to the count of four and repeat the whole process as many times as it takes for your mind and body to relax.

Blow your troubles away: In a comfortable position, inhale deeply through your nose, feeling your stomach inflate like a balloon. When your lungs are full, pucker your lips and exhale slowly as if you are blowing up a balloon. Blow up as many balloons as it takes to make you happy.

Practice, practice, practice!

Move along with the unicorns, and don't get your horn stuck in the mat. Try to hold each position for three to five full breaths. Don't be discouraged if you can't do it the first time, or even the tenth time. That's why yoga is called "a practice." Make it your own. But remember, the most beautiful pose always comes with a smile.

EASY POSE: a meditative pose that allows for reflection and stillness

CAT-COW POSE: a spine-strengthening pose that increases coordination and relieves stress

TIGER POSE: an energizing pose used to awaken the mind and body

CHILD'S POSE: relax the muscles and focus the mind in this resting pose

DOWNWARD-FACING DOG POSE: a calming pose to strengthen arms, legs, and shoulders

FORWARD-FOLD POSE: improve blood flow and promote healthy organs in this pose

PLANK POSE: a core-strengthening (abdominal region) pose that also builds strong bones

COBRA POSE: keep your spine flexible and increase lung capacity with this pose

UPWARD-FACING DOG POSE: a muscle-building pose for the back and upper body

RELAXATION POSE: complete your practice and get ready to move through the rest of the day in this rejuvenating pose

NAMASTE: a greeting that means "the light in me recognizes and honors the light in you"

CAT POSE

TIGER POSE

FORWARD-FOLD POSE

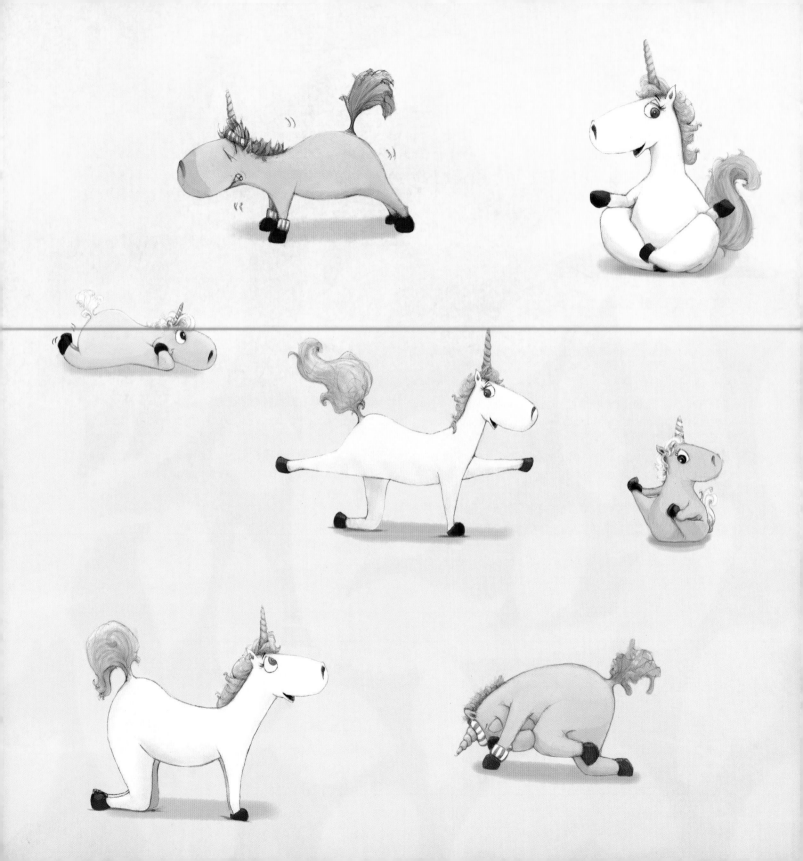